Marcus Fayette Bridgman

Mosses, Under the Pine, Seaweed

Tales at the Manse

Marcus Fayette Bridgman

Mosses, Under the Pine, Seaweed
Tales at the Manse

ISBN/EAN: 9783337089665

Printed in Europe, USA, Canada, Australia, Japan

Cover: Foto ©Andreas Hilbeck / pixelio.de

More available books at **www.hansebooks.com**

MOSSES,

UNDER THE PINE,

SEAWEED.

TALES AT THE MANSE.

A revised collection
of the poems of

MARCUS FAYETTE MAN.

To F. S. C.

I LOOK ACROSS THE YEARS

WHICH SEPARATE US,

AND OCTOBER SENDS A GREETING TO JUNE.

Of the poems originally printed in the volumes entitled "Mosses" and "Under the Pine," seventeen have been retained in the present collection, but not essentially changed in the revision.

CONTENTS.

I.

MOSSES.

First Poems.

2

Yet the amaranth
Above the rank soil blows,
Yet is the sunshine warm
Beyond the shadow of the cypress tree,
And yet beside the nightshade blooms the rose.

AFTER THE SUMMER.

THIS afternoon the autumn winds are silent,
Which crept so chill along the slope at morning,
And looks to-day so bare the lonely orchard.

At length has come the dreamy, sere October:
The daylight sleeps upon the noiseless upland,
And soft the haze that fills the voiceless valley.

A mile away, the river burns and glistens,
Through yonder willow gleams the distant village:
A shaft of fire above it flames the church-spire.

The woodbine listless droops about the window:
Nor stirs the maple by the quiet doorway,
And sheer against the sky leans the still locust.

As in my room I sit with busy fancy,
And thinking of the vanished days of summer,
Sings Zilla at her task a plaintive ballad:

> The landscape no longer is smiling,
>   The leaves in the woodland are sere;
> The note of the robin is husht,
>   And pale is the wane of the year.
>
> The lily blows not in the meadow,
>   The roses of summer are dead;
> The sparrows and kinglets have come,
>   But the thrush and the swallow have fled.
>
> But the thrush will come back and the swallow,
>   When the sun shall have melted the snows,
> To the meadow the lily return,
>   At length, to the cottage the rose.
>
> Yet the Spring to man's life twice comes not,
>   Not twice to its landscape its flush;
> Blooms the rose or the lily but once,
>   But once come the swallow and thrush!

Warm is the sunshine on the honeysuckle,
Beyond I catch the sight of sombre hemlocks,
And far-off glimpses of the dusty highway.

Below the vacant garden gleams the sumac,
White on the hillside are the leafless birches,
And wood and field proclaim the pensive autumn.

UNDER THE WILLOW.

A RUSTIC fence upon the slope,
    Not far beyond the orchard trees,
Surrounds a plot of freshest sward,
    A hillock mark'd by two white stones.

On the rich soil the clover blooms,
    So green is there the eglantine,
A willow by a headstone droops,
    And moss half hides the simple name.

In Elmer's field the mowers swing
    Their scythes below in rhythmic time,
And through the orchard comes the talk
    Of laborers in the curling corn.

Leans one against the fence hard by
    The peaceful spot and headstone pale,
As gently stirs the summer breeze
    The willow-tree and eglantine.

To-day the bramble bush is rank,
    Its ripe fruit glowing through the leaves,
And nodding near the wooden gate,
    It shifts its shadow on the wall.

" 'T was here we walkt one quiet eve
    The path beyond the ash," he said,
"And lingers over Wayland's wood
    In fancy still the sinking sun,

When friendships we recall'd so oft,
    Which then were dead with buried years,
And fortune's fickle change — but oft
    What ruthless Death from Time had won."

And swing with rhythmic strokes their scythes
    The mowers in the sultry field,
While through the orchard comes the talk
    Of laborers in the curling corn.

And swings the bramble in the wind,
        Its ripe fruit glowing through the leaves,
As nodding by the wooden gate,
        It shifts its shadow on the wall.

The sunlight sleeps upon the grass,
        The soft breeze steals along the slope,
The willow rustles o'er the mound,
        And near it rocks the eglantine!

DRIFT.

WE sat that evening in the yellow mansion,
As shone the glimmering firelight on the hearthstone,
And o'er the landscape glowed the autumn sunset.

And in the pauses of our talk our faces
Turned long and often to the narrow windows,
Where in the sunlight swung the restless woodbine.

Hard by the oaks were red among the pine-trees,
Brown were the fields of meadow land beyond us,
And burned the maple by the ancient doorway.

Gleamed in the glimmer of the waning daylight
The light spray of the restless surf below us,
And on the shore we heard the long waves breaking.

Beyond we looked so often to the lighthouse
Which rose so still and dark above the waters,
Or sometimes gazed upon the dusky headland.

While in the distance, as our eyes turned seaward,
We saw three white sails on the far horizon,
And over them the pale moon at its quarter.

Then as the evening stole so softly o'er us,
And faded from our sight the distant village,
The fields of autumn in the deepening shadows,

And in the twilight of the quiet landscape
The dark hills loomed beyond the silent meadow
So dim and vague to our imperfect vision,

Within was warm revived our ancient friendship,
The Past yet glowing from its half-dead ashes,
While in the fireplaec burned the dying embers.

3

THE NIGHT-WIND.

So darksome are your boughs, unquiet pine tree,
Within the mellow moonlight, and so heavy
Your midnight shadow on the summer greensward.

And over me where now I lie and listen,
I hear like whispers from mysterious voices,
The faint, low murmur of the fitful night-wind.

O pine-tree! so unquiet in the midnight,
And always in your sombre branches sighing,
Like some unhappy spirit earthward straying,

In all the burden of your constant sadness,
One plaint you have — 't is " Nevermore " and " Never,"
Whispers of Yesterday and of To-Morrow!

IN THE LAP OF EARTH.

HARD by the dusty highway of the village,
The ancient wall secludes the still inclosure,
A peaceful plot of earth, the village churchyard.

Not far from
the well-
worn road.

And near it stands the ancient church whose windows
On one side from the high and narrow casements,
Look silent o'er it with their panes so sombre.

Near it the
rustic fane.

Rank grows the grass beneath its solemn shadow,
So dense and wild on that dark soil the greenery,
And rank the elder by the gloomy gateway.

Luxuriant
is the
greenery
there.

And there
the bramble.

Across the wall luxuriant creeps the bramble,
And groups of children in the pleasant weather
Will often come to pluck its o'er-ripe berries.

About the
place
can be seen
an
evergreen,

And there you 'll see the red fruit of the eglantine,
With here and there a sad, low shrub of hemlock,
A stunted fir, a scarlet-colored sumac.

A willow or
an aspen.

Sometimes a willow or a scattered aspen,
A rosebush there which early blooms in summer,
On some low mound the green leaves of the ivy.

Many an
early
and later
flower.

There oft you 'll see the white flowers of the bindweed,
And every May the violet or the bellwort,
In later months the aster and the cinquefoil.

In autumn
the leaves of
the grape-
vine in the
birches
and locust.

The leaves yet glowing on the wrinkled grapevine,
In the bare birches and the leafless locust,
Or by the fence a lingering goldenrod.

Soft is
the twilight
there.

The shades of night upon the grass are falling,
Where yet a woman lingers in the twilight,
And through the plaintive silence steal these accents:

" Green is their turf, so green, who here are sleeping!
The hillock long be green where weeps the willow,   By
a hillock,
And twine the ivy round this quiet headstone.

Here oft be seen the king-cup and the daisy,
And ever on this spot the year's first violet,   A voice.
Here every coming autumn late the aster."

ON LOOKING AT THE PORTRAIT OF BURNS.

It flows, and blooms, and waves.

IN fancy winds the Doon and blooms the heather,
Still waves on Coila's sunny rigs the thistle,
And caller gowans deck the field each season.

The aspects of nature familiar to him, are pictured to the imagination.

There Spring its soft flush brings to all the landscape,
Looks fair on bonnie braes the skies of Summer,
And golden Autumn shines on fell and dingle.

Oft as these scenes return,

Oft as the light of morning gilds the upland,
Or in the shaw the Doon at mid-day lingers,
Or nightly sleeps the moon upon its bosom,

Oft as are heard in mellow days the voices
Of cantie harvesters within the ryefield,
Or talk of reapers in the bearded barley,

The reapers
and
the harvest.

Or lads and lassies gather at the hamlet,
In moonlight dance upon the leesome greensward,
Or in the gloamin chat beneath the hawthorn,

The moon-
light dance,
the chat
beneath the
hawthorn.

Or often as the cotter sits at even
With ruddy face before the glowing hearthstane,
And near, with quiet air, the gentle guidwife,

The cotter
sitting by the
fire, the
guidwife
hard by.

Or caddies clatter idly at the alehouse,
Or household tale is told by winter fireside,
Or carlin croons her song beside the chimlie,

Or caddies
clattering at
the hamlet,
or fireside
talk, or carlin
crooning
her song,

So long shall there each rural scene and pleasure,
Lang Syne to every Scot so oft reviving,
Recall the name of Scotia's rustic poet!

So long
Lang Syne
shall return,

So fresh his memory shall be kept forever
By every breeze that whispers in the bracken,
Or curls the grass beside each Scottish burnie,

So fresh
shall be kept
the memory
of Scotia's
poet.

By every
breeze that
rustles
the barley.

·By every wind that sways the summer thistle,

Or stirs the heather on the lonely moorlan,

Or gently rustles in the bearded barley,

So fresh his
memory
shall be kept
in cottage
and hamlet.

By every lad and lassie at the calchan,

In every dance upon the leesome greensward,

In every cottage by the lighted ingle!

BONNIE, beautiful.
BRACKEN, fern.
BRAE, a bank, a declivity.
BURN, BURNIE, water, a rivulet.
CALLER, fresh.
CANTIE, cheerful, merry.
CLACHEN, a small hamlet.
CLATTER, to tell little, idle stories.
COILA, a district of Ayershire.
COTTER, the inhabitant of a cottage.
CARLIN, a stout, old woman.
CHIMLIE, a fireplace.
CADDIE, a young fellow.
DINGLE, a dale.

FELL, a level field on the side or top of a
   hill.
GOWANS, daisy, dandelion, hawkweek, etc.
GLOAMIN, the twilight.
GUIDWIFE, the mistress of a house.
HEARTHSTANE, the hearthstone.
HEATHER, the heath.
INGLE, a fireplace.
LASSIE, a young woman,—a girl — applied
   particularly to a country girl.
LEESOME, pleasant.
RIG, a ridge.
SHAW, a small wood.

ONE EVE.

WELL, here, at even, o'er the gate I'm leaning,
By the still way that leads to yonder village,
Whose panes against the western sky are gleaming.

And from the Past one far-off eve is shining,
So warm in fancy is a vanished sunset,
When all the air was genial with the spring-time:

When the light breeze of evening wooed your tresses,
And heavy was the air with orchard perfume,
With odors of the lilacs and the pear-trees:

4

When half in shadow lay the vale beyond us,
And half the elms below were toucht with sunshine,
While at our feet the shallow streamlet lingered:

When long we talked of the bright days of summer,
Which soon would bring the field-sparrow to the upland,
At length the wood-thrush to the silent forest.

And here, at even, o'er the gate I'm leaning,
While now, I think, so softly sleep the shadows
On one pale stone among the quiet willows!

II.
UNDER THE PINE.

Here, as I sit beneath the pine-tree,
    Which sighs and moans,
Awake within my soul the echoes
    Of its low tones.

THE LIKENESS ON THE WALL.

HERE is her portrait o'er the marble bust,
And oftentimes upon the silent face
I gaze, when I am in a musing mood.
I 'm sure you 'll say the countenance is fine.
The quiet eyes are fair and full of thought,
But mild and dreamy as an autumn day.
The forehead is not high but beautiful —
The brows, I think, are delicately arch'd,
The nose as rare as Ariadne's.   Yes,
The skill of Valentine so well has limn'd
The lineaments.   See, now the hair looks warm,

30   *Under the Pine.*   Poem I.
The Likeness
on the Wall.

Which falls about the temples, lending half
Its lustre to the neck in this soft sun
That through the casement gleams.   And sometimes here
I linger in these quiet days an hour
Before this portrait.   The original,
At rest, lies in the classic soil of Rome,
Hard by the pyramid of Cestius.
It is a still, secluded spot on which
The turf, moist with the soft Italian dew,
Each year is green.   The violets blossom now
Upon it every Roman winter.   There
Might one sleep well.

         Quite true, you 'll trace, I think,
Some features in the physiognomy
And mine — a family resemblance — but
The likeness is not marked.   Younger than I
By fifteen years, one mother had we both,
Not the same father.   Of a gentle nature —
Of better mould, indeed, than common clay,
'T is ever thus that I recall her.

                                 I
Remember well — 't was only three short months
Before we laid her in her Roman grave —
One cloudless evening of an autumn day

We sat upon the Palatine, and saw
The clear sun set — as all the Sabine hills,
The summits of the distant Apennines,
With crimson glowed and purple, till at last,
The lingering sunlight through the ancient trees
Fell on the ruins at our feet, and stole
The deepening shadows over all the scene.
There as we sat beneath the cypresses
And watched at times the evening star,
As one by one the silent hours slid by —
Long talk'd we of that path our feet had trod,
And oft of what had been, but what would be
No more forevèr — of the mystery
Of Life, and ·how the glory of the world
Doth fade, while Faith and Love remain.
There as we sat beneath the cypresses
And watched the evening star — as on her face
The moonlight fell,—"A few short months,"— she said,
"And this frail frame of mine will quite succomb,
This transitory dream be o'er — and here
Amid the shadows of a twilight Past,
My sleep be calm even in an alien soil."
And through the solemn silence then we heard
The convent bell upon the Cœlian Hill
Tolling for midnight orisons.   Ah, sir,

How often with the memory of her,
Comes back the hour!
              So mellow falls the light
Upon the face! There something you will learn
Of that fair spirit whose remembrance still —
Through every year — is fragrant in my soul.

A MILL–IDYL.

The Mill.

IF, when you go toward Landis Green, you turn
A short half-mile this side the noiseless vill,
And cross the low-arched bridge that spans the brook,
Where leans a clump of alders o'er the bank,
You 'll see beside the smooth and narrow way,
A dozen rods beyond the babbling stream,
Behind a locust and a sycamore,
The mill — and scarce a rod above it where
The willows, rank with ooze and moisture, droop
Above a shallow pond.   In summer days
A pleasant and a dreamy shade is cast

5

Along the by-road and about the mill,
And on the bosom of the quiet pond.
There by it every year the spearwort blooms,
And at its margin flames the marigold,
While bars of golden light the water streak,
And through the leaves the warm west glows, whene'r
The sun is low.   You mount the great stone step,
Across the ancient well-worn threshold pass,
As swims the light dust in the beams that steal
Through the dim window-panes.   And there the sound
Of grinding swells the hazy air within,
Which shakes the heavy cobwebs as they hang
About the windows where the huge flies buzz
And die.   Therein so oft on cloudless nights
The silent moon looks wan.   And window-frames
There rattle with a melancholy sound,
By gusty night-winds stirred.   Then sway the long,
Lithe willows in the moonlight, and no more
The tranquil shadows sleep, but wildly dance
About the lonesome spot, and sleeps no more
Within the wrinkled pond the midnight sky.
In at the eastern window faintly peers
The morn.   And half the long warm afternoons,
Through the great doorway burns the westering sun,
And creeps the shade athwart the dusty panes,

As swift the swallow flits about the eaves,
Or sits the blackbird in the alder-bush
Hard by o' noons within the sleepy run.

The Miller.

The world is old,
And the burden theeof,
But the phoebe swings
In the reeds to-day,
On the water-way.

Thinks the miller as he
By the hopper stands,
"So long have spun
The mill-stones round,
As the grain I 've ground!

Yet the great wheel turns,
And the mill-stones spin,
And still I grind,
By the hopper here,
The grain each year.

So the seasons go,
While to-morrow brings
The selfsame task,
Till the wheel at the mill,
And Life stand still."

INSIDE THE GATE.

You 'll see it near the ancient gateway,
But a rod from the low, dark pine —
I cannot tell how many summers
    Has bloom'd over Alice
      The clover.

It can be scarcely less than twenty
Since the willow was planted there —
And many autumns I remember
    Has swung by the headstone
      The aster.

It can be scarcely less than twenty
Since the eglantine nodded there,
And waved above the spot the daisy —
    Or crept o'er her bosom
        The ivy.

And so beyond the ancient gateway
But a rod from the low, dark pine,
To-day the earth is over Alice,
    And leans o'er the footstone
        The yarrow.

LOW–TIDE.

" Was it the Sea ? "

He askt
if it was the
tide.
He asked —

And far off broke the tide.

The words

In slow and faltering speech he spoke.

I gazed upon his countenance so pale,

Then out into the soft midsummer night.

" It is the tide

I said
it was the
tide,
Which breaks below

Upon the solemn shore," I said —

" The never-resting waves

That o'er the shingly beach

Breaking
on the
shore,
Are breaking on the midnight strand "—

And stole the moonlight

Through the woodbine
Which the faint air scarcely stirr'd —
"There shines upon the Sea
The mellow Moon,
Which at the dawn will yonder set so warm!

Yes, it is the tide,
The breaking of the surf upon the shore,
The moaning of the main beneath the full-orbed Moon!"

Beneath
the
Moon.

Was it the Sea?
Or broke the tide of Life so low?
So calmly broke the tide of Life,
So low in Death's deep silence there.

Was it
the
Tide?

And at my window,
Looking out between the vines
Upon the moonlit bay,
As long I lean'd against the panes—
I heard no sound but of the Sea.

I lean'd
against the
panes,
and heard
only
the Sea.

SEAWARD.

On the shore I stood,
By the ebbing tide,
Faintly on the long beech breaking.

And afar I saw,
On the deep, blue main,
Three ships slowly sailing seaward.

Three ships in the sun,
O'er the deep, blue main,
Toward the summer sunset sailing.

Till I saw them sink,
Slowly dipping low,
To the golden gates of evening!

Ah! the ships that go
Over Life's wide main,
Time-borne barks returning never —

Will ye furl your sails
Yet in calmer climes,
Keeping still your courses seaward?

NEPENTHE.

So silent is the room — so husht and dim —
Where nothing breaks the stillness but the sound
Of our low voices — and the sombre gloom
Is pale with that scant light which yonder steals
Through close-drawn curtains and the darkened panes.
And yet why speak in undertones, or shut
The sunshine out? The ear of Death is cold,
Nor would the eyes that closed at yester-eve,
Be dazed by this May morn. So fair, say you?
Not Life itself could ever give to her
The beauty which this marble paleness does,
This marble-like repose. The quiet brow,
The calm and long-lashed lids, the lips, their sweet
Expression keeping yet, the dark-brown hair
Which softly falls about the pleasant neck,

Are passing fair.   You can but mark, I 'm sure,
The chin so finely modeled — while the cheek,
Where scarce you see the ravage of disease,
Is in its wanness beautiful with that
Stray lock upon 't.

               To-morrow they will bear
Her hence, and lay her loveliness away
Beneath the shadow of the aspen-tree,
By yonder church.

              They 'll well perform their task!
Alas, too well, as they will coldly heap
The clods upon her there.   And then I 'll wish
The earth that covers her would cover me.
If I could lie within the quiet grave
Which shall forever hide this lifeless form,
I 'd closely press the clay-cold face to mine,
And think Death lovely, for I 'd rest, I know,
In blessed peace with her.

                So by the church
They 'll break the turf to-morrow, at the morn.
Yes, in the faint, gray daylight of the dawn.

AGNES.

'T WAS by an altar, in an ancient church,
At Michaelmas, a maiden prayed for death —
And this the prayer she prayed so earnestly,
Low-kneeling there before the crucifix:
"O Son of Mary, who art pitiful!
The freshness and the greenness of my life
Is gone — and oft my breath is but a sigh.
I am as one who sits in cheerless days
Above the dead, dry mould of summer fields,
And hears the mournful autumn sigh — or hears
The bleak winds wildly wail in all the woods
Of Spring. So dreary and so joyless seem,
Alas, all days to me, from morn to eve,

At length this boon I ask — that I may taste
The sweetness and the blessedness of death."

The hoar frost came, then went the wintry days,
And warmer breezes stir the maple leaf,
The bramble-berry ripens by the wall.
Late is the hour, and scarce the wandering wind
Disturbs the hush of yonder lonely spot,
When underneath the silent summer moon,
She with a lover in the churchyard walks.
Why seek the two the churchyard lone and still,
Or there rewalk the grass-grown path so oft,
Where headstones glisten in the moonlight pale?
Below the quiet moon they tell their love,
And plight their troth beneath the cypress tree!
And so All-Hallows' soon should make them one,
The two be wed within the ancient church,
That stood with ivied walls and tower thereby,
Where once the maiden knelt, at Michaelmas,
And prayed before the crucifix for death.

All-Hallow night; for months have come and gone.
Dim burn the lights within the ancient church,
While in the west the waning moon is wan.
So dense the throng, that scarcely there is seen

The haggard sexton's form, whose grave hard by,
Within the shadow of the gloomy fir,
To-night is green — or hers, the withered belle,
Who died so long ago, or that frail form
Which so sepulchral looks amid the crowd,
On whom in autumn late the aster blows
Each year — or hers, with face so blanch'd, who pass'd
One early morn from earth, and yonder stands
Before the picture of the risen Christ —
Or hers, the maiden by a lighted shrine,
Whose eyes on yon Madonna oft are bent,
Who faded like a rare and fragile flower
One far-off June — or scarce is noticed hers,
On earth a castaway, who gazes long
Upon the likeness of the Magdalen —
Or hers, on whom the grass is rank, who turns
So often to the painting on the wall,
The martyrdom of St. Sebastian —
Or hers, within the twilight of a niche,
Whose life went out upon her wedding-day,
On whom each spring has waved the guelder-rose —
Or hers, the fair bride once, but standing there
With countenance so white against the panes,
Who faded with the orange-bloom she wore,
And lies to-night beneath the eglantine!

Lo, up the aisle the bridegroom and the bride
To the high altar walk.   And there, as sets
The waning moon, and tolls the midnight bell
Within the ivied tower — the twain are wed.

And closely to his breast he presses her,
In his embrace!   Then o'er her features stole
A mortal paleness — while in low, faint tones,
As when a breeze is dying in the pines,
She breathed these words in slow, expiring breath:
" Sweet is thy kiss, and yet thy lips so cold! "

THE CHURCH BY THE GREEN.

Yet stands the church by the village lawn,
And looks so dim o'er the churchyard still.
    (Death, the reaper, gathers his sheaves!)
About the windows the woodbine crawls,
      And creeps o'er the eaves.

By its walls the leaves of the locust are green,
And green is the ash by the low church door.
    (Leaves grow sere, like the hopes of men!)
The swallow builds in the belfry its nest,
      In the gable the wren.

And tolls for the dead each season still
The sexton old the churchyard bell.
    ("Ah!" he says, "dies the bloom on the flower!")
And a peal far out he rings each day
      From the ivied tower!

THE LAST REQUEST.

I 'D hoped that I might see another morn,
But, doctor, ebb 's the tide with me.   The pain
That rack'd my side is gone, and now my brain,
Which was a whirling world of cloudy thoughts
At last is clear.   I 've something on my mind
I 'd say, before the tide goes out.   You 've done
What you could do, but well I know, too well,
I 'll never in the good ship Neptune make
Another voyage.   Ah, sir, closer come,
Or you 'll not hear.   If you 'd but take the load
From off my chest which makes my breath so short —
But no, you cannot — if you could, I 'd try

7

To speak above this faint, low tone.   Come close,
For I must make you understand.

O, yes,—

At Inveran I said she lived, hard by
The Galway coast.   It comforts me to think
That I shall never know one bitter tear
She 'll shed for me.   No, long this sleep will be,
I 'm sure, and then I shall not heed her tears.
What sound is that?   Is it the low night-wind
I hear a-moaning hoarsely in the pines
In yonder yard?   I thought it was the gale,
And we 'd been struck by some no'theaster.

So

The message, doctor, I 've not told you yet?
Here is a locket with her miniature.
This with the message send her, that to-night
My thoughts ofttimes went back to her, and say,
Why, say the voyage ended in a calm,
At last, after rough weather.

But a bell

I hear.   The clock's which strikes the hour of twelve,
Say you?   I thought it was a knell — and toll'd
The fate, at last, of some poor comrade.   Well,
No clay-clods pile on me when I am dead —
They 'd press me down — the earth would lie

So like a stone upon my breast I could not sleep.
Ah! 't is low water and the tide will not
Come in.   Two mornings when the ship leaves port,
Make me a shroud o' the ship's sail — and then
Let some short service or a prayer be said —
And be my grave the wide, the wide, wild waves —
The bosom of the all-embracing sea.

A REVERY.

THE time, the place, I think, are now so distant,
It was an August eve, as I remember,
And we were sitting on the quiet grass-plot.

So gently o'er us stole the night's slow shadow,
So faint the lamp-light through the casement glimmer'd,
So lightly in our ears the woodbine rustled.

So long we sat and watched the distant lighthouse,
The far-off village and the dusky headland,
So long the river flowing darkly seaward.

So oft the languid night-wind stirred your tresses,
So long our hands were claspt in that still starlight,
So low and earnest were the accents spoken.

So mellow'd is the scene as I recall it!
As when upon a tranquil night in autumn,
The moon on some far field is softly shining!

III.

SEAWEED.

Some seaweed strewn upon the shore,
Where breaks the tide of Life forevermore.

A GLEAM OF MEMORY.

THE hour I well recall,
The pleasant lawn, the vacant way,
Before the porch the ancient fir,
The room wherein I sat with her,
The flower-piece on the wall,
The sunset flush
That softly shone between
The quiet vines,
As stole the dreamy hush
Of evening over all the scene.
And I remember still
When the warm light went out above the hill,

And through the ivy faintly gleam'd
The lamp hard by within the sacristy,
So long across the fields we looked
Upon the moonlit sea.

Yet in the hush
Of summer eves,
Warm glows and dies the sunset flush
Among the honeysuckle leaves,
And in my fancy one,
Within the shadows of the silent room,
Though over her the summer grass is rank,
Still fixes oft her wistful look on me,
Then gazes through the moonlit air
Across the shimmering sea!

THE SEXTON.

I 'm thinking, sir, I know it, every rod
And foot of ground hard by, and I have been
The sexton here for many a year, I 'll say,
And made the graves here'bouts.   Well, yes, the place
Is getting pretty full of mounds.

                            He stood
Beneath the locust-tree and lean'd across
His spade.

        You see that headstone green with moss,
Between two smaller ones beyond the path.
I well remember when Job Randall went
To his last home.   'T was in a nipping air,
' Faith, it was in the bitter wind of one
December day.   He 's never minded much
The weather since I laid him by the wall.

    8

You see the grave a few rods from the gate,
Where falls the shadow of the bramble-bush,
O' afternoons, upon a low, white stone.
Seth Peters I remember well.　'T was on
A sharp mid-winter day I buried him
Beneath the snow.　But snug he 's laid, I 'm sure,
In yonder spot since then.
       There at your left,
The third one in the row, my friend, I call
A handsome slab.　'T is not a score of years
Ago I heap'd the earth on 'Lijah Lane.
Old 'Lijah, may be you have never heard
Of him, and you 're a stranger in these parts.
But in the mansion over there he lived,
Where you can see the sycamore.　He had
A deal of money when he died, and hugged
His gold.　Yet little has he, but enough
To-day, a tombstone and that patch of ground.
Just there the headstone at your right, may be
A rod from youder ash which shades the path,
I used to think, too, was a handsome slab.
But o'er it yearly creeps the the dull, gray moss,
Which almost hides the name of Walter Clare.
Folks said he was a poet.　All I know,
He sometimes walked about the village street,

Yet oft would wander through the fields and lanes
Alone in pleasant weather, sit for hours
Beside a brook and listen to the sound
It made among the alders.   Once it was,
A bright June day, that by old Lockwood's mound
He lingered as I broke the greensward there,
One afternoon.   " 'T is not so poor a spot
To rest in when one lays his burden down,"
He said.   Just then the shadow of the church
Had touched the grave beyond.   The robin sang
A pleasant song upon the aspen-tree.
And here the poet, too, was brought one day,
Before the next year went.   But by the ash
So early blooms the king-cup over him,
So late the aster and the goldenrod.
I like to see a willow by a grave.
'T is not so gloomy as your fir or pine,
And casts a pleasant shade.   The willow-tree
Is green to-day where waves the eglantine
On Ellen Archer's grave.   Ah! she was young,
A lily, sir, that faded summers since.
So rank is there the grass!   Yet as I lean
Across my spade, still young I fancy her,
As when it was a pleasant sight to see
Her face at church upon a Sabbath morn,

Or hear her sweetly sing the evening hymn.
Too young, too young and fair to die, I thought.
'T was when I saw her cold, fair face, and placed
A single rose-bud in her snow-white hand.
Then at the funeral they sung the hymn
I 'd heard her sing but three short months before.
The other day, 't was but the other day,
I stood a half-hour by her hillock. You
May be will think it strange. But somehow, friend,
The thought of her fill'd both my eyes with tears.
I know the dead forever are at rest.
The young who die sleep well, and sound the old,
In this still spot. Yes, yes, the young lie down
At morning, but the old, I 'm sure, are glad
To reach the goal at night. There 's some that say
A churchyard is a lonesome place. To me
It is a kind o' pleasant spot. And here
I often think I 'll knock at Life's last inn
At night-fall, when the weary day is done.

THE SOUL'S ECLIPSE.

THE seasons pass,
And yet so much from all the world is gone,
Since the one hour
Which I recall, alas!
There is for me no glory of the dawn
Or mid-day, or of setting suns
Or starlit night,
Nor beauty of the flower
Or summer grass,
Or shadows sleeping where the winds are still,
Nor music to my ear of purling rill,

Nor calm delight of solitude
Within the pathless wood,
And glows no more the golden haze
That fill'd the quiet autumn days.

The months go by apace,
Abides with me
But Memory.
Henceforth one hour shall unforgotten be,
The hour I looked on Death's pale face.

THE RECONCILIATION.

So long a while, remember, we 've been friends.
It 's nigh two score of years that you 've known me,
And I 've known you, James Strong.   I see your farm,
And you see mine.   Hard by is both to each,
Between them but a scant half-mile.   And we
Were friendly neighbors not three months ago.
I 'll own my temper sometimes is too quick,
And some hard things the other day I said
Of you, at Foskett's.   Let them pass.   Old friends
Should be old friends.

      I never was the man
To envy your prosperity, James Strong.
Why should I?   Yonder farm of moderate size
I call my own, and where 's the man will say
To-day I owe him aught?   But you, you look

Each morning from your doorway there on your
Two hundred acres.   Citizens are we
Of whom the people of this goodly town
Speak well.   We 've had enough of angry talk
About a paltry bit of pasture land.
Well, yonder is the horse I bought of Rugg,
Above a year ago, the dappled gray.
The animal has some fine points, you see,
A handsome leg and neck, a head I call,
Mark you, a beauty.   Body not too long,
But well-proportioned, and an eye I like.
And there 's the dark-bay horse beyond the roan.
I bought him when a colt.   No animal
With fancy points, you see, and yet there 's not
A better roadster than the bay.   But come,
The horn has sounded.   Now the dinner waits.
So no excuses, you shall dine with me,
When we 'll discuss a sirloin roast, the crops
And markets, try the wine which Kate has made.

THE TWO TRAVELLERS.

WHERE the sunset glows through the leafless top
    Of a single sycamore tree,
From the sunburnt edge of the short, crisp grass
    The path creeps down to the sea.

Here as I sit by the cedar-copse
    In sight of the summer grain,
Breaks on the hazy air so low
    The moan of the distant main.

9

Beyond upon the shadowy cliff,
    I hear at times the jay,
While yonder traveller's steady pace
    Plods over the lonely wav.

But I will watch the warm light wane
    Till the day to its goal has run,
I will seaward go at the voice of the sea,
    And follow the track of the sun!

THE MAN OF BOOKS.

You see those sycamores.   He lives thereby,
And has resided, stranger, many a year
In that square mansion.   Little does he stir
Abroad, but spends his days among his books,
And, sir, he has no end of books.   Year in,
Year out, he reads them, and 't is wonderful
How much there is of learning in his head.
You 've heard of cyclopedias, and yet
He is a library in himself, my friend.
Ah, well, he knows a deal about the men
Who lived so long ago.   One afternoon,
'T was at the mansion but the other week,
He learnedly discoursed an hour or more
Of ancient times, and much he had to say
About the famous days of Greece and Rome,

The mighty things which then were done, he said,
By Alexander, Caesar, Hannibal,
And others in the by-gone ages, sir.
I say, it is amazing, hearing him
Discoursing of the orators of old.
He handles them like any scholar.   Yes,
He 's just an ancient with the ancients.   All
The greatest orators are ancient, sir,
At least, so he has often told me.   Quoth
He, 't was the afternoon that I have said,
"Ah! tell me, what 's your modern eloquence,
Compared with that of hoar antiquity?"
And he will talk you by the hour, perchance,
About Demosthenes or Cicero.

You see the gateway.   Yonder is the house.
You 'll find him there behind the sycamores.

TO DEATH'S MESSENGER.

TEMPT him with pleasant tones,
Allure him like the soft and gentle night,
From the oppressive, garish light,
The ways that men with weary footsteps tread,
To thy serene abode
Where comes surcease of sorrow,
And they who weep to-day will sleep to-morrow.
Entice him with sweet speech,
Win him to thy still realm
Where storms are husht,
Where winds are lull'd as at a summer eve,
Where the harsh sounds that pierce the day
No more are loud,
And wrap the darkness round him like a shroud.

AS HE LEANED OVER HIS AWL.

I STICK, sir, to my last, and keep my shop.
Here at my work I 've sat, my shop I 've kept,
For many a year.   No stopping place, I find.
Drops in the parson of an afternoon
To chat with me, and no one better likes
A joke than parson Dale.   In other days
Old Leonard here would come to sit an hour,
Talk of the weather and the crops, rehearse
The gossip of the town.   No more the door
He opens now, nor in the village street
His face is seen.   I recollect the time
They bore him to the churchyard on the hill.
Well, yes, mine is an honest trade, I say.
And yet, my friend, I do not occupy,

You know, the first seat in the synagogue.
There is 'Squire Anderson, up the broad aisle,
At church, he walks, the sexton with a bow
Shows the pew-door to him, and when he speaks
To men, they reckon it an honor.   Folks
Are proud to shake the hand of lawyer Ladd,
Not mine.   Yet mine, sir, is an honest trade.

AFTER THE WRECK.

AT the edge of the wind-blown pines,
The fisherman's cottage stands,
Down by the beach,
And the long, straight reach
Of the white sea-sands.

Sits in the cottage one
Gazing far over the main
Toward the quietly setting sun.
And there by the window-pane
Is a child with a sweet, sad face,
That wistfully
Looks out on the rippling sea.

" Not to-night, alas !
He comes not to-night,"
The mother says, with a sigh,
And the fair child weeps,
And the mother gazes over the waves
With tearful eyes at the sunset sky.

But down by the beach
And the long, straight reach
Of the white sea-sands,
To the fisherman's door
Comes the fisherman no more.

AT THE BURIAL.

At length, with heavy steps,
They bear him to his rest,
One with the weight of life oppress'd.
The pallmen slow
Their burden through the gateway bear,
And up the churchyard go.
There is the fresh, damp heap of earth,
In it is thrust the sexton's spade,
With which, at morn, the grave he made.
But soon the final words are said.
They slowly lower the dead,
And when all rites are done,

The pallmen, one by one,
Walk out of the shadow into the sun.

Wanes the summer day,
Shine the headstones cold.
At sunset from the churchyard gate,
Went the sexton old.

THE TWO WAYS.

'T was at the parting of the ways we stood,
And goes the by-way there
Across the level lea,
The other by the silent wood.

We parted at the parting of the ways,
That never could for us be one,
And since so far apart our paths have run.
There winds the homeward way,
The other o'er the lea
Forever to the deep blue sea!

IV.
AT THE MANSE.

Here fall the rays of Memory on the fields
That once were green,
Like moonlight in a tranquil autumn eve,
Upon a far-off scene.

PREAMBLE.

HALF a mile beyond the vale,
Where the highway climbs the slope,
White with orchard bloom in May,
Near the weather-beaten church,
With the shadow of its spire
Stealing o'er the grassy graves,
Looks the mansion through the trees
Still across the vacant street.
Heavy is the perfume there
Of the lilacs every spring,
And beside the silent path
Blossoms yet the guelder-rose.
Ancient is the lonely Manse,
With its faded yellow walls,
And its roof with moss is green,
And the sombre window-panes,
Where the daylight steals within,

Half are hid by mantling vines,
While the honeysuckle creeps,
Rank about the sleepy porch.

There as seasons come and go,
Distant is the outer world,
Life itself a quiet dream.

Lingering in the frosty years,
In the twilight of the Past,
In the dim, wainscoted room,
Sits a wrinkled, white-haired dame
And relates these simple tales,
As I tarry for a night,
Late in summer, at the Manse,
On my walk from Stokeley Green.

As here through uneventful days I sit
Amid the shadows of my lengthen'd life,
I think of hours so oft that are no more.
And o'er the Present, like a setting sun,
The light of Memory ever softly glows!
I still remember well, I say, the time,
It must be now two scores of years ago,
The season Edward Randolph led his bride
From yonder church. 'T was when the locust-tree
Was scenting still the air of June. She wore
A wreath of smilax, and six wild-flowers in
Her hair. Ah, sir, to-night how fresh and fair

They look, through forty years, as I recall
The scene! As fresh and fair was Mary Lane,
As any flower that day. And all the scene
Comes back to me, as 't were but yesterday.

Two miles away within a sleepy dell,
There is a little rustic bridge that spans
The brooklet slowly slipping through the run,
And where the sunshine scarcely steals at noon.
The crowfoot every summer lightly swims
In the dark waters of the silent stream,
While o'er the channel leans the celandine
From the moist margin which is rank with sedge.
And every season rocks the willow-tree
Across the bridge where creeps the narrow way.
The path crawls upward from the lonely run
Through birches and a growth of underbrush,
Winds through a copse of stunted oak and pine,
And then descends a gentle slope to join
A by-road, shaded oft by ash and elm.

Well, yes, so many times the path I 've trod
To Mary's doorstep, when the orchard slopes
Were white, or days were balmy with the first
Spring buds. And still behind a pleasant yard
11

That blossoms every May with snowballs, where
The rosebush blushes by the path in June,
Where morning-glories half the windows hide,
Looks the small doorway on the by-road near,
In autumn skirt with yellow goldenrod.
Twelve years had whitened yonder button-wood,
Each May, since tidings of the Falcon sunk
In Bengal Bay the story told how half
The crew with Randolph, master of the ship
Which foundered off the isles of Andaman,
One mournful day went down, as outward bound
It voyaged from the coast of Hindoostan.
To-night I recollect the afternoon
So well, when Edward's fate in Bengal Bay,
At length was but a scarce repeated tale,
As Mary and myself together sat
Within the same neat cottage by the way,
Whose threshold she had crossed as Randolph's bride.
Again the orchard blossoms scented all
The air, and heavy was the perfume yet
Of lilacs in the yard.   Then while his song
The bobolink across the grassland sent,
We caught the sight of neighboring fields, the brook,
The slope hard by, the wood beyond.   Meantime
We turned the leaves of Memory o'er and o'er,

As toward the by-gone years we look'd where some
Had kept for us their freshness still.   " Sad breaks
The sea forever on its sands," she said,
" One word repeating ever, Nevermore! "
"And yet," I said, " to-day the fair sun shines,
The vale is rich with orchard bloom, and fresh
With scent of lilacs and of snowballs, all
The air so fragrant with the balmy life
Which still the spring renews.   So hearts may break,
And dead hopes rustle like the autumn leaves
With a sad sound beneath our feet — for us
Shall Nature smile, and woo us oft to its
Deep peace — and Hope, and Joy, and Faith, and Love,
Shall make the present and the future still
So rich with golden days.
                              And then, at length,
We both sat silent.   Well, I thought the years
Had changed her since her wedding-day.   So cslm
Her face in its pale beauty, and the eyes,
O'ershadowed by the pleasant lids, at times
Were instinct with a quiet pensiveness.
A sweet expresaion had the countenance,
But it was thoughtful, and thereon I saw
The shadow of an unhealed grief, as when
A cloud darkens still water.

"True it is,"

She said, as o'er the pleasant fields awhile
She gazed, "that Nature woos us oft to its
Deep peace.   Yet oft to broken hearts, Hope, Joy,
And Love, are empty words.   With me the Faith
Remains — and Peace — but not the Peace which Time
Or Nature brings to wounded souls."

                     Beyond
The Manse, in later months, the sumac leaves
Are red beside the churchyard gate, and shines
The scarlet hazel every year hard by.
Not distant from the path that yonder runs
Between the crowded, grassy graves, there is
A moss-grown stone.   The poplar o'er it waves
Each year, where blooms the goldenrod, and glows
The ripe fruit of the eglantine.   The mound
Is eastward of the middle path, and o'er
The marble creeps the vine.   There half the name
Perchance the eye will read.   The bramble leans
Against the footstone where the children come
To pluck its berries oft in summer-time,
The hawkweed and the aster in the short
Autumnal days.   And oft the bluebird sings
In the gray aspen, in the mountain-ash
The oriole.   So many times I've heard

The linnet in the willow there, and once
The redstart in the solitary pine
That sighs above the low, dark wall.
                              I 've sat
An hour sometimes by that still mound, or lean'd
Across the headstone.   In that silent earth,
So peaceful is the sleep of Mary Lane.

I saw upon old Elinor's pale cheek
A tear.   She bent her head in silent thought,
Then buried deep her face within her hand.
But Myra toucht, at length, the harpsichord,
And to its music sang a quiet song:

>   When shall Time its solace bring,
>   For the hopes that fade to-day?
>   In the yellow year?
>   Will it warm the autumn fields,
>   When from Life the summer goes,
>   And the leaf is sere?

>   When shall Love in calmer days
>   Fairer be than fairest flower?
>   In the yellow year?
>   When the blush of June is gone,
>   When the bloom has left the rose,
>   And the leaf is sere.

So died the song of Myra on the ear,
As in the dusky room we silent sat,
And on the dame I gazed in thoughtful mood.
She raised her head, but spoke not, as she looked
Through the still woodbine at the moonlit sky,
And soon again began:
           In yonder vale,
Where two low willows drink the sluggish stream,
And spans the bridge the brook, the still road turns,
Creeps through a copse of maple, then by one
Low sycamore before a silent lawn.
Behind the lawn that every year is green
When the low sycamore is bare, and fields
By autumn frosts are brown'd, a mansion stands,
Whose walls are mantled thick with clambering vines.
The windows ever have a gloomy look
Where sleeps the heavy honeysuckle shade
When no winds stir. The straight and smooth-flagg'd path
Between the flower-beds from the gateway runs
To the worn footstep of a sombre porch,
While one lone locust leans against the eaves,
And steals its shadow o'er the ancient roof,
As sinks the sun. Each year the yard with grass
Is overgrown, the shrubbery untrimm'd,
The flower-beds oft are choked with summer weeds,

And scarce the window-panes are visible
Through the thick greenery. So dimly Day,
Between the curtains and the dark-leaved vines,
Illumes the solitary, spacious rooms,
Or peers on cloudless nights the mellow moon,
Where Hester Heyne, sole heir
And tenant of the mansion, sits or glides
Amid the shadows of a distant Past.
Her face is thin, and snowy-white her hair,
Her features wrinkled, but there lingers still
A waning lustre in her mild, grey eye,
And light is still her step — her form as yet
Erect, or scarcely by the strong years bent.
Yes, long do I remember her as old —
A lonely woman with a high-bred air,
And with the manners of the olden time.

There often as the noiseless seasons go,
She spectre-like within the twilight walks,
Or near the great high window keeps her seat,
But sometimes in the lonesome later years,
Stands thougntful by a portrait on the wall.
The likeness is of him who in her youth
Her fresh heart won, but died upon the day
They would have wed. The face, which still survives

The dull and cankering tooth of Time, is young,
With pleasant lineaments and handsome mouth,
And lustrous eyes, and finely moulded chin.
The hair, of chestnut hue, in wavy lines
Falls to the shoulders, and the brow is fair.
Ah! when upon the canvas streams a ray
Of golden sunshine, all the countenance
Is life-like, where the lips forever seem
About to speak.   From a small casket nigh,
Long kept within an antique cabinet,
She takes a single, slender, dark-brown lock,
Whereon she gazes in her revery,
Yet from it she will often cast her glance
To the still portrait.   But, at length, the lock
Replacing in its alabaster case,
She slowly shuts the cabinet and sits,
Her face deep buried in her hand for hours
In silent thought.

                    I know not if the dead
Ever come back to earth, or if they do,
Can be by human eye discern'd.   Yet so
It is affirmed, and manifest themselves,
At times, to our gross sense.   Perhaps they do.
For who can tell what mystic ties may link

The spirits of the Unseen World to this?
But I, indeed, believe if from their sphere
They can to mundane scenes return, they must
Revisit oft the earthly haunts they loved.
Who knows but sometimes they are visible
To mortal sight?
     'Tis said, that as the time
Comes round that should have been her wedding-eve,
Old Hester for her lover patiently
Her vigil keeps. All night she is arrayed
As for a bridal of the olden days,
In costly but half-faded dress, and rich
Adornments of a fashion worn no more.
The story runs that at a certain hour,
Alighting from a spectral carriage near,
A manly form ascends the large stone steps,
The threshold crosses, entering the room
Without a footfall where old Hester sits,
As bride for bridegroom waits. And noiselessly
With scarce a gesture, it will seat itself
Beside the aged, withered dame. The lips
Oft move as if in speech, but do not speak.
The features are of one in early life,
Fair-brow'd, with many a dark-brown lock, the **face**
Yet handsome, but the countenance is pale,
  12

The eyes lack-lustred.   Its allotted space
May stay the speechless and mysterious guest,
The still, strange visitor.   But when the clock,
Which heavily ticks out the fleeting hours,
Strikes twelve within the dimly lighted hall,
The form departs, while not an echo breaks
The silence — crosses with a noiseless step
The threshold — quits the mansion — then is lost
In moonlight or the viewless air!
                         Hard by
The breeze sighs in the single cedar-tree,
And year by year the one lone locust leans
Against the ancient eaves, and ever there
Are mystic whispers of the night and day.
And I have heard that oft on summer nights,
A wandering strain of fitful melody
Will through a window and the clustering vines
Steal softly on the silent air.   So wild
And yet ethereal it seems, but dies
At times, or on the silence swells, like some
Rare harmony.   At length, the strain will cease,
And quietly a feeble voice will sing
Some snatches of a half-forgotten song,
Or simple ballad to a plaintive air,

Which once, perchance, was often heard in days
Of yore.

          The thorn-tree by the garden stands,
Where creeps the grapevine o'er the wall, and rank
The poppy grows beside the path that runs
Between the beds of marjoram and rue,
To the low grass-plot by a lonely tarn.
Thereby you'll see a button-wood and one
Sad fir, whose roots have deeply struck within
The darksome soil, and o'er the margin lean
The willows.   Blossoms every summer there
The trumpet honeysuckle, every year
The marigold and celandine.   The sun
Scarce lights the waters where the pickerel-weed
Crawls from the reedy bank.   The owl will sit
In the high hollow of the button-wood
From the first flush of morn to dusky eve,
And hoot, yes, often in the moonlight pale,
Or in the moonless gloom.   Ah, sir, the place
At night-fall is a spot which persons shun.

And plaintive were the words which Myra sang,
As then her fingers toucht the harpsichord:

Long we talk'd of autumn days,
Oft of golden sunset skies,
And the quiet words she spoke
In my ear are lingering yet:
" Southward soon the swallow flies,
But erelong with Spring returns,
In the Spring will you forget? "

Warm the field beyond me lies,
Blooms to-day the guelder-rose,
And the honeysuckle blows,
While the swallow northward flies:
Swallow, you may bring the Spring,
One the May will not restore,
Nor the Spring forevermore.

" She will not wake," said one,
   " More still her sleep, at last,
Than low winds husht at eve,
   Whose pain, we know, is past."

Fresh stole the early air
   Across the summer corn;
The night had brought her rest,
   Nepenthe at the morn.

Long has the small house yonder overlook'd
The orchard, where the well-worn pathway runs
To Dawson's mill.   And from the wide highway
Which climbs the slope to meet the silent street

A little lane between the hedges leads
To the still cottage.   Thence the eye may catch,
Above the orchard and neglected hedge,
A distant prospect of the vale below,
The winding brook that steals between the elms,
The peaceful meadow-lands, or upland farms,
With rustling grain-fields glistening in the sun.

Well, no, the cottage is not far away,
Just up the shady, sleepy lane hard by.
There lives the white-hair'd miller, there has lived,
I 'm thinking, now two score of years or more.

And I remember at this hour so well,
The miller's daughter.   Pleasant is her face
As I recall it, and the hazel eyes
Are full of tenderness, and fair is yet
The brow.   What matters it if she has lain
For years beneath the aspen-tree ?   The dead live oft
In Memory, and my thoughts are in the Past
To-night.
             It was, but it was autumns since,
Upon a Hallowe'en, and in the rites
Yet practiced at that superstitious eve,
 T was said she saw a lover's handsome face,

A mask, a coffin, and a snow-white stone.
And thinking of the face which she beheld,
Within the mirror of the darkened room,
She laughed.   Nor ceased the giddy merriment
Until the bell within the ivied tower
Of yonder church toll'd forth the midnight hour.

That night like other Hallowe'ens had gone,
And often was recall'd to mind the scene,
Whose rites had once evoked the mystic signs
Of Love and Death.
                   And in the course of time
The maiden's love was won, to her were pledged
The hand, the faith, the troth of Edward Earl.

The months went by, the seasons passed, a year.
But toward her lukewarm grew his heart.   And still
At times, the two would walk the orchard path
In pleasant afternoons, or twilight grey,
Or sometimes loiter in the quiet lane,
Or sit an hour beside the cottage door,
As softly waned the light of setting suns.
October came ere long with mellow days.
He went more seldom to the cottage.   Yet
Less frequent.   Then, one evening at the gate,

He press'd her hand, and said a calm " good by."
The " good by " coldly fell upon her ear,
And woke a mournful echo in her soul.
So fickle was her lover, it was said.
Nay, nay, but false the heart of Edward Earl.
One night, old Montague, the sexton, sat
Late in the sacristy, I 've heard him say,
As through a window shone the summer moon.
And while he gazed upon the headstones near,
He thought how often he had ply'd his spade
And laid the dead to rest hard by.   And oft
He thought of them he 'd brought to slumber there
Since the wild wintry night he last had rung
The old year out, the new year in.
                                    " So fast
The hour-glass runs," he thought, "the years slide by!
At best life 's but a span.   And well I know
The travellers reach the self-same goal at last,
Where all roads meet.   To-night old Floyd sleeps well.
So sound by yonder locust Roger Rand.
To-night the grass beneath the willow-tree
Is green on Nancy Gavin's grave."
                              The breeze
Stole o'er the sexton's cheek, but scarcely stirr'd
The ivy at the casement.   Softly gleam'd

A moment in the west a setting star,
But lower'd o'er Langley's wood a gloomy cloud.
And gazed old Montague upon the scene,
The landscape glimmering in the moonlight pale,
Where vague the valley in the distance lay,
While far along the warm horizon loom'd
The dusky outlines of the silent hills.

But white the headstones in the churchyard gleam!
As in the sacristy the sexton sits
Buried in thought.   But in the low church tower
The bell, at length, the hour of midnight tolls,
And wakes him from his revery.   The tones
Die on his ear, and faint the lamp burns yet
Upon the table.   Did he fancy it,
Or did a face peer on him through the vines,
A woman's face, a woman's figure glide
Among the tombstones, hasten down the path,
And straightway vanish through the churchyard gate?

The grass grows rank by Dawson's pond, and low
 The willows o'er its margin lean, but bloom
The honeysuckle and the celandine,
The wild rosemary every summer there.
Dark is its water in the moonless nights,

And silent is the gloomy water-way,
As oft the beetle whirs among the reeds,
Or sometimes when the days are long, the crow
Will sit within the solitary ash
Hard by, or near it in the button-wood,
Half-dead at top, the blackbird watch the sun.

Still is the mill, and still the water-way,
And cool the shadows sleep in Dawson's pond.
They slowly bear her from the water's edge,
The miller's daughter, on the morrow when
Above the willows broke the morning light.
Yes, slowly in the early morning air
They bear her lifeless up the narrow path
That winds among the ancient orchard trees,
To yonder doorway where the woodbine hides
The miller's cottage.   Ah! her grave was deep,
In quiet water.
                    And beyond the church
They gently laid her, but with many a tear,
A few rods from the churchyard wall.   And when
The sexton broke the fresh turf for her grave,
At morn, 't is said the raven thrice he heard
Above him in the grey light of the dawn.

13

Yet blossoms over her the goldenrod,
Each year the daisy.   Late in autumn once
I pluck'd an aster from her peaceful mound.

So ran the tale that Elinor rehearsed,
And thus the words, at length, which Myra sang:

Yes, often I recall the summer hour,
When slowly walking on the sandy shore,
We paused, at length, beside the restless sea,
And said, " So far apart our paths would be,
That hence would not be one forevermore."

And softly o'er us shone the sinking sun,
That toucht the hills beyond the quiet lea,
And as we lingered by the solemn main,
We knew how wide apart our paths would be,
Which never, never could be one again.

We parted at the spot,
    Where I am lingering yet;
The words, long since, we spoke,
    Remains the vain regret.

The vain regret! the fault
    To-day I clearly see;
We miss'd the flower that bloomed
    But once for you and me!

Yes, I remember one to-night who lived
At Stokeley Green, a score of years ago,
The rare musician.   Often I recall
The pale Annette, his only child, and scarce
Seventeen, his sole companion.   Other kin
The man had none.   Born in a foreign land,
By masters taught in Germany,
He was himself a master of his art,
And played his violin with such a skill
That few could equal it beyond the sea,
Much less in all the region hereabout.
Annette, (she always seemed to me so frail,)
Not little of old Herman's genius had,
And none who ever heard her sing forgot
Her voice, for marvelous I thought it was,
And lingers in my memory yet despite
The lapse of time.   You 've heard in some deep wood
The thrush, as you have lingering stood to catch
Its clear, ethereal strain, that charmed at times
The stillness and your ear.   Such the young girl.
She was the thrush indeed that charmed all ears.

A gentle nature ever I remarked
In her.   Mild were her darkly hazel eyes
That always had a dreamy look.   Her face,

I say, as I have said, was pale, yet were
The features beautiful.

      Scarcely was heard
The music of the old man's violin,
But with it Annette's voice.   And villagers
Whene'er they went along the way at night,
Would often stop to listen to her tones,
The strains of his rare instrument.

        The face
Of Annette paler grew as months went by,
And yet a brighter lustre had her eye,
Her voice lost nothing of its marvellous tones,
But more and more ethereal they seemed,
Evoking strange, unearthly harmony,
Like that the air from some Æolian harp
Breathes on the ravish'd ear.

       "She must not sing,"
The old physician said to Hoff one day.
"Too weak the girl to exercise her gift
Of song.   I know whereof I speak.   Her hold
On Life is by a slender thread.   So bid
Her for the present sing no more."

        And went
The summer, came the mellow days,
With the sere leaves of autumn.

It was one
October night. The wind was up. The vines
Against the window-panes and casement swung,
The broken clouds across the sky were driven,
Obscuring oft the moon. And fitfully
Upon the lawn, from Herman's cottage, shone
The lamp-light through the restless honeysuckle.
Then was it that along the chilly air,
At length, to ear of villager, were borne
The strains of the musician's violin,
The rare tones of Annette. 'T was said the notes
Were from a famous foreign opera,
Composed by some old master. Hour by hour
Ceased not the strains, against the windows toss'd
The woodbine in the gusty wind, the rack
Across the moon was driven. More rapturous
The music grew of Herman's violin,
The tones of Annette's voice. And still the light
Flares from the narrow casement on the lawn,
As from it still the rapturous harmony
Floats on the autumn breeze. But suddenly
It ceases. Nothing breaks, at last, the hush,
The solemn stillness of the lonely room,
But the wild night!
        So quiet was her sleep

102   *At the Manse.*   Tale IV.
The Musician and his
Daughter.

At morn — a dreamless sleep. Look'd warm the sun
At noon through rifts of golden cloud.

                      They bore
Her through the churchyard gate, and laid
Her by the locust, ere its yellow leaves
Were shed.

         'T was said, that afterward, at night,
From yonder cottage could be often heard
Old Herman's violin and Annette's tones.

        Gently broke the languid tide
        On the strand beyond the lea —
        Faded from their sight the ships,
        As they watched the sinking sun,
          Sitting by the sea.

        Went at length the sunset flush,
        Stole the shadows o'er the lea —
        Heard the quiet listening moon,
        But reveals no words they spoke,
          Sitting by the sea.

And ceased the music of the harpsichord,
The voice of Myra on the listening ear.

www.ingramcontent.com/pod-product-compliance
Lightning Source LLC
Chambersburg PA
CBHW032158010726
47493CB00008BA/2744